Benjamin's Book About To, Two and Too

COPYRIGHT © 2017

BOLD NEW LIFE PUBLISHING, LLC

Boldnewlife.com

ALL RIGHTS RESERVED

ISBN: 1-947280-02-3
ISBN-13: 978-1-947280-02-1

Benjamin is very excited **to** go **to** school and learn.

He has **two** teachers and a wonderful classroom. Sometimes, the boys and girls think they get **too** much homework, but Benjamin likes doing homework. Out of all his homework, Benjamin likes reading the best. He likes his teachers and his classmates, **too**.

Each day, Benjamin and his classmates go outside during recess **to** play on the playground.
The playground has **two** sets of swings, monkey bars and two slides.

Sometimes, when it rains, it is **too** wet **to** go out and the children have **to** play inside.

The children have puzzles, board games, and building blocks **to** play with. Sometimes, the Teachers help the children paint or color. Benjamin likes to paint and color, **too**. Today Benjamin colored three cool pictures.

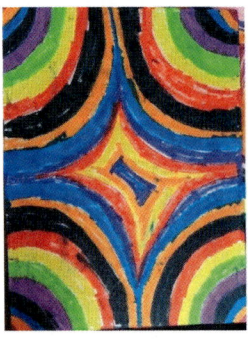 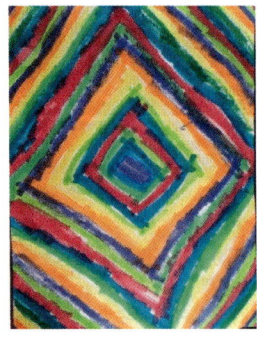 

All the children learn **to** read, and they like **to** visit the library **to** check out all kinds of books. Every Wednesday is "Library Day" for Benjamin's class. The children all look forward to ten o'clock when Mr. Stephens says, "Line up, it's time **to** go **to** the library!" Sophie checks out **two** books.

Benjamin checks out **two** books, **too**.

One of Benjamin's books was about **two** bears that went to the river for a swim. The **two** bears swam for a while and then relaxed on the smooth river rocks. Benjamin wished he could go **to** the river **to** swim and relax on the smooth rocks, **too**.

The river reminds him of the time he and his brother went fishing. The blue-green water looked so cool and relaxing he wanted **to** jump right in!

On Fridays, the children bring food **to** make creative "Fun Friday" snacks. Benjamin always brings something **to** share with the class. One Friday, the children had **too** many marshmallows.

Another Friday, they had **too** much peanut butter.

Every day after school, Benjamin goes home. He has **two** dogs named Alex and Luke. Luke is a spaniel that has been around since before Benjamin was born. Alex is a German Shepherd who is only four months old. Alex is full of energy and loves **to** play ball. Luke likes **to** play ball, **too**.

Sometimes, Alex has just a little **TOO** much energy and plays with things he is not supposed **to** play with. One day, when Benjamin was playing badminton with his brother and his dad, Alex caught the shuttlecock and ran off with it. Everyone laughed and yelled as they chased Alex around the yard. Luke was chasing Alex, **too**.

Benjamin has a big brother named Joseph. They love animals. Other than their dogs, they have **two** guinea pigs and a cat, **too**. They would have a whole house full of animals and reptiles, except their dad said no more.

The **two** brothers are learning how **to** take care of the animals. They check **to** see that they all have food and water. Each of the animals requires different care. Dad told the boys **to** take turns keeping the guinea pigs cage clean. Sometimes, they take the dogs for a walk. Alex loves going on walks. Luke likes walks, **too**.

In the evening, after a long day of learning and playing on the playground at school, Benjamin gets ready for bed. Before he goes **to** sleep, his dad tucks him in and reads **to** him from his **two** favorite books. Benjamin often tells his dad, "I love you", and his dad tells him, "I love you, **too**!"

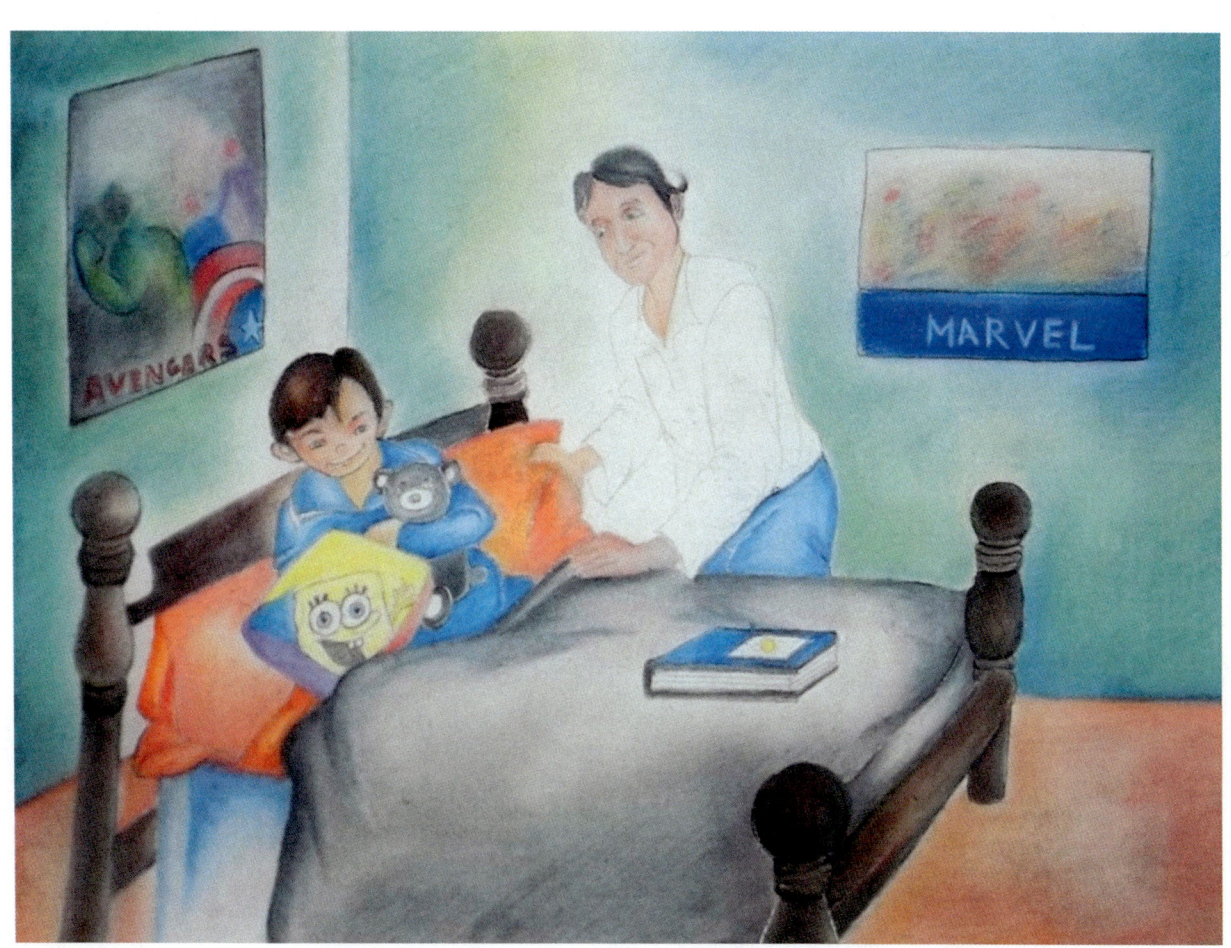

Author Bio
Scott Adcock

I was born October 5, 1961 in Clovis, New Mexico and moved to Mississippi when I was two. I began working and making my own money at only 10 years old by delivering newspapers on a motorcycle to about 200 homes every day before school. Since then, I have worked consistently all my life, and have never been without a job. I bought my first house when I was 17 years old. I currently have four children, three boys and a girl. I enjoy carpentry, woodworking, painting and growing flowers, mostly Zinnias. I believe the word of God more than I believe what I see.

COPYRIGHT © 2017

BOLD NEW LIFE PUBLISHING, LLC

Boldnewlife.com

ALL RIGHTS RESERVED

ISBN: 1-947280-02-3
ISBN-13: 978-1-947280-02-1

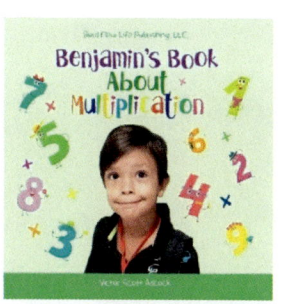

Made in the USA
Coppell, TX
23 November 2021